Time AND AGAIN

*by a click of the clock
you can go in reverse
time and again
for better or worse*

BY ROB CHILDS

ILLUSTRATED BY NICOLA SLATER

Librarian Reviewer
Kathleen Baxter
Children's Literature Consultant
formerly with Anoka County Library, MN
BA College of Saint Catherine, St. Paul, MN
MA in Library Science, University of Minnesota

Reading Consultant
Elizabeth Stedem
Educator/Consultant, Colorado Springs, CO
MA in Elementary Education, University of Denver, CO

STONE ARCH BOOKS
Minneapolis   San Diego

First published in the United States in 2007
by Stone Arch Books,
151 Good Counsel Drive, P.O. Box 669,
Mankato, Minnesota 56002.
www.stonearchbooks.com

Originally published in Great Britain in 2005
by A & C Black Publishers Ltd,
38 Soho Square, London, W1D 3HB.

Library of Congress Cataloging-in-Publication Data
Childs, Rob, 1950–
    Time and Again / by Rob Childs; illustrated by Nicola Slater.
    p. cm. — (Pathway Books)
    Summary: Thanks to a mysterious old watch, Becky and her twin
brother, Chris, travel back in time, but the novelty soon wears off as they see
the consequences of their interference in past events.
    ISBN-13: 978-1-59889-116-4 (hardcover)
    ISBN-10: 1-59889-116-2 (hardcover)
    ISBN-13: 978-1-59889-271-0 (paperback)
    ISBN-10: 1-59889-271-1 (paperback)
    [1. Time travel—Fiction. 2. Twins—Fiction. 3. Clocks and watches—
Fiction.] I. Slater, Nicola, ill. II. Title. III. Series.
PZ7.C4418Tim 2007
[Fic]—dc22   2006005085

Art Director: Heather Kindseth
Graphic Designer: Kay Fraser

1 2 3 4 5 6 11 10 09 08 07 06

TABLE OF CONTENTS

Chapter 1

TIME TO GO

"Fetch, Tan!" Becky threw the stick across the field and the dog raced after it, barking in excitement. This was Tan's favorite game. She picked the stick from a clump of grass, and ran back with her prize.

"That didn't go very far." said Chris with a laugh. "Girls can't throw!"

"Okay, so you throw better than me, little brother," Becky said, teasing her twin, as she often did, that she was ten minutes older. "But I can run faster."

Chris didn't argue with that. His sister could outrun everybody in their class.

"It's my turn," he said, taking the stick from Tan's mouth. "Bet I can reach the river from here."

The stick whirled through the air with the dog yelping after it. Both ended up in the water. Tan scrambled onto the bank with her prize clamped between her teeth. She shook herself, spraying thousands of drops into the air.

"We better head back home," said Becky, hearing the church clock strike four times. "Come on, Tan!"

The dog bounded toward them.

Staying away from the railway line that ran around the town of Barnwell, the twins continued to play with the dog. Chris slipped a leash on Tan.

Tan tried to tug Chris along a little quicker than he wanted to go. There was some schoolwork waiting for Chris at home and he was in no hurry to get back. "Let's take a look at the market," he suggested.

Becky turned to stare at him. "Since when have you been interested in the flea market?"

Chris ran a hand through his hair, a sign that he was uncomfortable. "Well, you never know what you might find."

"I know you," said Becky with a grin. "You haven't done your homework yet, have you?"

Chris shrugged. That was the trouble with having a twin sister. She always seemed to know what he was thinking.

"No sweat," he grunted in response.

"I've got plenty of time," he added.

"No, you don't," said Becky. "You promised Dad you'd help him restock the shelves."

Chris groaned. He forgot about that. The Jackson family ran the local store and their parents insisted that the twins should help out. "Can't you do it for me tonight, sis?" he begged.

"No, it's your turn. I did my work earlier, cleaning the counters."

Chris let out a heavy sigh. "Oh, well. All the more reason for not rushing back. Let's check out that flea market."

They made their way to the town square. Becky stopped at a booth that was selling clothes.

Then Chris spotted a familiar, dark-haired figure walking toward them.

It was Luke. Chris saw enough of Luke at school. They sat at the same table in class, though not by choice. His mom had caught Luke trying to steal candy from the store more than once. She called him a born troublemaker.

"Funny meeting you here!" Chris said. "Come to see what you can steal?"

"I don't steal stuff," Luke protested. "So leave me alone. And take that ugly mutt with you."

"Tan's beautiful," said Becky, giving the dog a little pat.

"I wasn't talking about the dog," said Luke, delighted his joke had worked so well.

Chris's reaction caught Luke off guard. Chris pushed him in the chest so hard that Luke stumbled back against one of the tables, making it wobble.

"Hey! Get out of here!" shouted the man who owned the booth. "I don't want you kids disturbing my customers."

"What customers?" snorted Luke. He glanced at the clutter of items on the booth table. "Who'd want to buy any of this junk?"

Luke snatched an item from the booth, and then ran out of the market.

"Hey! Come back with that watch!" the man cried, but Luke had already disappeared.

So had Becky. Still annoyed by Luke's insult, she was chasing after him. She was followed by Tan, who had yanked the leash out of Chris's hand.

It was a little while before Chris caught up with them. Guided by the noise of Tan's barking, he found them in an alley, where Luke had tried to hide behind a large dumpster.

When Chris arrived, Luke dropped the watch into the dumpster. "You want it, you get it," he told the twins. "I'm out of here!"

Chris looked at his sister. "You or me?" he said, knowing the answer.

"You." Becky grinned. "I've got Tan."

Chris opened the lid of the dumpster. "Pheeewwwww! It stinks in there!"

It was lucky that the dumpster was almost full, since it would have been difficult, and very unpleasant, to reach down to the bottom.

"Wish I had some gloves," Chris muttered. He held his breath while he looked carefully through the rotting junk.

"Any luck?" asked Becky.

Chris grunted, just as his hand grabbed what felt like a chain. He pulled it out to discover that it was attached to a silver watch.

"Got it!" he cried in triumph. He dangled the watch high above Tan's sniffing nose.

Becky took it from him, using her sleeve to wipe some mess off the glass. "It looks like a stopwatch with these buttons around the dial," she said. "It must be pretty old, though. It's even got Roman numerals."

"I didn't think the Romans had watches," Chris joked.

Becky turned the watch over in the palm of her hand and saw there was some writing on the back. It was in the form of a short rhyme. The small squiggly script made it hard to read.

"Strange," she said. "I wonder what it means."

by a click of the clock
you can go in reverse
time and again
for better or worse

"I have no idea," said Chris, leaning on her shoulder to peer at the words. "I'm no good at poetry."

"'By a click of the clock,'" she read. "Hmm. Well, let's try this button at the top first and see what happens."

Becky pressed down the red button above the XII.

Click!

They were both standing in the field by the river again, with Tan wanting the stick to be thrown for her to fetch.

The twins stared at each other in disbelief. The only thing that was different from before was that Becky now had a watch in her hand.

"What are we doing back here?" Chris asked. "This is crazy!"

Chapter 2

TIME SLIP

"I don't understand," Becky said. "What happened?"

"I don't know," Chris said. "It doesn't make sense."

Tan was not bothered by the strange event, and just wanted to play. "Quiet, Tan!" Chris ordered her to stop barking.

Feeling a little dizzy, Becky sat down next to the dog. She petted Tan's smooth black coat and white neck.

She needed to know that this was for real and not a dream, or a nightmare.

"Good girl," she said. "It's okay."

"It's not okay," Chris said. "It's not even close to okay. We're supposed to be in town, not in the middle of a field!"

Becky looked at the watch. "The last thing I remember doing was pressing this red button."

"Well, don't do it again," said Chris. "Give it to me." He reached out for the watch, but Becky refused to hand it over.

"'By a click of the clock,'" she said, repeating the first part of the writing on the watch, "'you can go in reverse.'"

Chris shrugged. "So?"

"So I think that's what we did. We went backward in time," said Becky.

"And here we are, standing by the river again," she added.

Chris stared into the distance toward the clock on the church tower.

"The clock says it's 3:30," he pointed out. "And we heard it strike four earlier, remember?"

"You mean later," Becky corrected him. "It hasn't actually happened yet."

Chris slumped to the ground beside his twin. This was getting strange. Tan tried to lick his face, but Chris pushed her away. "Dumb dog! Get down."

"Don't take it out on Tan," said Becky. "She only wants some attention. She doesn't know what's going on."

"Well, that makes three of us, then," said Chris.

"We must have slipped back about an hour," said Becky, "but things aren't exactly the same, are they? We weren't having this conversation before."

Becky examined the watch more closely and noticed a separate dial in the lower left corner of the face. Inside, was a little gold arrow moving slowly.

"Look at this," she said, holding out the watch for her brother to see.

"There's a tiny extra hand, and I bet it's ticking off the hour we're repeating."

"So what do we do now?" asked Chris.

Becky thought for a few moments. "The first thing we should do is go back to the market and return this watch. It's not ours."

"Not yet, but it will be."

"How?" asked Becky.

"We'll buy it," said Chris, grinning.

"Oh, no, we won't!" Becky jumped to her feet in alarm. "It's too dangerous."

Chris snorted, refusing to listen to her concerns. He walked toward the town, eager to reach the market before Luke appeared.

He had no idea how this whole time business worked, but he did know one thing for sure. He wanted that watch.

"Wait!" Becky cried, jogging along with Tan to catch up with him.

"What's the matter now?" he said sharply.

"Have you thought about this?" asked his sister.

"What do you mean?" Chris asked.

"What I mean is, how can you buy something that isn't there?" she said. "The owner probably doesn't even know it's missing yet."

That made Chris stop. "I guess we'll just have to smuggle it back onto his table first," he replied, "and then buy it."

Against her better judgment, Becky agreed to help Chris. She distracted the owner with a question about one of his items for sale while Chris pretended to lift the watch out of a box.

"Um, how much is this?" Chris asked.

"How much you got, kid?" replied the owner, crossing his arms.

Chris fished into the pocket of his jeans to see what was left of his money. He found two dollars.

"Is that enough?" he asked hopefully.

The man shook his head. "Make it three and it's yours."

Chris looked toward Becky, who sighed and gave him the extra dollar.

"Thanks, sis," he said, grinning. "You won't regret it."

"Famous last words," said Becky.

Chris paid the money. Then he dragged his twin and Tan away from the booth before the man could change his mind.

"What a bargain!" Chris laughed. "He hasn't got a clue what this watch can do!"

"No, and neither do we," Becky said. "We don't know what we might be messing with."

"Messing with?" said Chris.

"Yes, messing with Time, with a capital T," she told him. "It's asking for Trouble. And that's got a capital T, too!"

Chapter 3

TIME IS MONEY

"Look lively, son. You're half asleep."

"Sorry, Dad," Chris said. He seemed to spend most of his time apologizing to his parents. He shook his head and looked around the store.

"Got something on your mind?" asked his father.

Chris smiled to himself. He didn't want to explain about the Timewatch, as he had started to call it.

He was so eager to use it, though, it was almost burning a hole in his pocket.

"Just some work I still have to do for school, Dad," he said as an excuse, glad that the watch could now give him any extra time he might need.

"You should've done it earlier like your sister did," said his father.

"Sorry, Dad."

"Now get those cans finished and then put the cereal boxes over there," Dad told him, pointing to an empty shelf on the other side of the store.

Chris continued to stack the cans of soup, tomatoes, and beans on the shelf behind the main counter. He made all the labels face the front. "If folks can't see it, they can't buy it," Dad always said. "Jackson's Second Law of Selling."

Chris deliberately put a can of chicken soup the wrong way around. He wanted to see how long it would take his father to notice.

"Give me a hand, Chris. I need you to hold these steps steady while I reach that top shelf," said Dad.

"I don't know why we have stuff way up there," said Chris. "Nobody can reach it."

"All they have to do is point," said Dad. "Remember the fifth law?"

"Um, if folks want it, we get it. Right?" said Chris.

"Right!" said Dad.

Dad put his weight on the rickety wooden stepladder and climbed up halfway.

"Isn't it time we got some new steps, Dad? These always wobble."

"If they were good enough for your old granddad, they're good enough for me," Dad told him.

Chris wondered how many of the laws on Dad's list had been passed on by Granddad. He gave a yawn and thought he might make his own list of things to do with the Timewatch.

He could use it to retake a test and fix any mistakes he'd made. He could double the time of gym class. He could replay a soccer game if his school team was losing.

At home he could delay bedtime by an hour.

"Aaargh!"

Dad's shout and the crash of the steps brought Becky, Mom, and a barking Tan rushing into the store. Tan reached Dad even before Chris could scramble over the broken tangle of wood.

"Are you all right, Dad?" cried Chris.

Dad groaned as his wife propped him up against a cabinet for support.

"I think I broke my leg," he moaned, his face wrinkled in pain.

"What happened?" asked Mom, her own face white with shock.

"It was my fault," Chris said. "I wasn't holding the steps right."

"No, you were right," said Dad. "Those steps are too old. I should've gotten rid of them years ago."

Becky crouched beside her father, stroking his arm for comfort. "What were you doing, Dad?" she asked.

"Stretching too far. Down I went."

"I'm really sorry, Dad," said Chris, as Mom went off to call for an ambulance.

"Nothing you could have done, son!"

"Maybe," Chris said to himself. "Or maybe not."

"But there is something I can do now."
He took out the Timewatch and glanced
at his sister, who nodded her approval.

Click!

Chris suddenly found himself in the
stockroom an hour earlier. He picked
up a box of soup cans to take into the
store, knowing exactly what Dad was
about to say.

"Get started on those cans, Chris.
Time is money, remember. Third law. I
don't want to be here all night."

"No, and I bet you don't want to
spend it in a hospital either," Chris
mumbled under his breath.

As Chris started his chores again, he
was planning how to prevent the accident.

Chris still remembered to put the can of soup the wrong way on the shelf to test his father's powers of observation. He also took the chance to go and tell Becky about the stepladder.

"Why didn't you travel backward with me?" he said, almost angrily.

"I didn't even know you went," she replied. "It hasn't happened yet."

Chris nodded slowly. It all seemed very confusing. "It just shows how useful this watch is," he said. "You know, the way it can let us stop people getting hurt, for instance."

"Of course," she agreed. "As long as we only use it in emergencies."

"Depends what you mean by emergencies," said Chris, slowly.

Becky looked at him suspiciously.

"And just what do you mean, little brother?" she asked.

Chris turned away to avoid having to tell Becky about all the things on his list, like having enough time to finish his homework, or retaking a test.

Working more quickly this time, Chris was already stacking the cereal boxes when Dad called him over to help.

"Give me a hand, Chris. I need you to hold these steps steady while I reach that top shelf."

"Isn't it time we got some new steps, Dad?" Chris said for the second time.

"If they were good enough for your old granddad, they're good enough for me."

That was the cue for Chris to take some action.

Before his dad could climb the steps, he jumped up onto them and deliberately made them wobble.

"Be careful!" said his father.

The steps tottered and then collapsed, but Chris was ready. He jumped off and rolled across the floor so the steps wouldn't land on top of him. The crash brought everyone running, as before.

A noisy Tan was soon on the scene, licking Chris's face. "Get off me, you dumb dog," he cried, struggling to get back on his feet.

"Are you all right?" asked Dad.

"I'm okay," Chris said, putting on a brave act, but giving Becky a sly wink. "Just a few bruises, that's all."

"What on earth were you doing?" asked Mom.

"Just doing my job," he said. "You know, trying to help Dad."

Dad sighed. "You were probably right about those old steps. We should've gotten rid of them years ago."

"I've been telling you that, too," said Mom. "If it had been you who fell off them, you might've broken your neck."

"Or a leg," added Becky.

"Right. Come into the kitchen, Chris," Mom told him, "and let me take a look at that arm."

"Oh, just one thing before you go, Chris," said his father.

"What's that?" asked Chris.

"Turn that can of soup the right way, will you?"

Chris grinned. "Sorry, Dad."

Chapter 4

EXTRA TIME

"What's this?"

"Uh, it's my homework, Mr. Samuels," said Chris.

The teacher held up the dirty, crumpled sheets of paper for the rest of the class to see. "It looks like something the dog dragged in," Mr. Samuels said.

Chris turned red as he felt all eyes turn toward him. Luke's laughter was louder than anyone else's.

It was true that Tan's wet paws had walked over the top page that morning when it had fallen onto the floor at home, but the real damage had been done by Luke.

Before class started, Chris had been sorting through the pages when Luke snatched the papers from him, crunched them into a ball, and then tossed them into the waste basket.

"Sorry, Mr. Samuels," Chris said, running a hand through his hair.

He did not want to tell on Luke. He wasn't the type, and Luke knew it.

"I should think so, Christopher," said the teacher. "But being sorry isn't enough. You will have to stay in at lunch and write this out all over again."

Luke chuckled. "Serves you right," he whispered across the table. "And I am not done with you yet."

Chris glanced across the room at Becky. She was the only person who wasn't laughing at him. He wished now that she hadn't talked him into leaving the Timewatch at home that morning.

"Who wants an extra hour of school?" she had said to convince him that she was right.

Becky had a point, but Chris could have gone back an hour and made sure that Luke had no chance to get him into trouble. Now Chris would have to miss the lunchtime soccer game.

Chris tried to be quiet for the rest of the morning. Luke, however, had other ideas. He kicked Chris under the table, making him yelp in pain and surprise.

"Was that you making that noise, Christopher?" demanded the teacher.

"Sorry, Mr. Samuels."

"Sorry, Mr. Samuels," mocked Luke out of the corner of his mouth.

"Please be quiet," said the teacher. "Some people are trying to work."

Luke laughed. He kicked again, but Chris was ready for him. He grabbed Luke's foot and yanked him off his chair.

Mr. Samuels put the blame on Luke this time. "You can join Christopher during lunch," he told him.

Becky drifted by their table a few minutes later on her way to the other side of the room to put a book on a shelf. "You boys having fun together?" she said, smiling.

The fight between Chris and Luke continued for the rest of the day.

Mr. Samuels left the room for a minute, and returned to find Chris and Luke fighting on the floor. He gave them both extra homework. During the afternoon, he had to stop them from flicking pencils at each other across the table.

The teacher's patience finally ran out and he sat the boys in separate corners of the room with strict orders not to move for the rest of the day.

After school, most of the students took part in the soccer practice.

The students were divided into four groups, and Luke was delighted to find himself playing against Chris in the first match.

"Always coming back for more, aren't you?" said Luke. "When are you going to realize you're useless as a goalie?"

That hurt.

Chris knew that the regular goalie, Butch, was better than he was, but he certainly wasn't useless. And he certainly wasn't in the mood for any more insults from Luke.

"Well, you won't score against me in this game," Chris boasted.

Luke laughed. "We'll see about that."

Both boys were determined to outdo each other. Chris was saving everything that Luke's team could fire at him. Luke was trying too hard to score.

"Don't be greedy," called Mr. Samuels, the coach, when Luke kicked another ball straight at Chris. "You should have passed to somebody in a better position."

Luke scowled. The only thing that mattered right now was getting the ball past Chris, and time was running out. Much to his relief, Luke finally managed to poke the ball into the net from close range.

"One to zero!" Luke cried. "I'm the winner!"

"That does it," Chris muttered under his breath. "I really will come back for more now. We're going to play extra time!" He excused himself from practice, telling his teacher that he wasn't feeling very well.

As soon as he was out of sight, though, Chris broke into a run and didn't stop until he reached home.

Luckily, his parents were busy in the store. He entered the house, slipped up to his room, and got the Timewatch.

Click!

He transported himself back one hour through time. "Hmm, maybe that wasn't a great idea," he thought, finding himself sitting in a corner of the classroom again. "I came back too far."

During the warm-up at the start of soccer practice, Chris managed to talk to Becky. "I'm back," he told her.

"What?" she replied, concentrating on her stretching exercises. "You didn't go anywhere."

"Yes, I did. I went home."

She realized what that meant. "I thought we agreed not to bring that thing," she said angrily.

"I needed it for an instant replay," he said, grinning.

Sadly for Chris, the grin was soon wiped off his face. The game followed a different pattern.

When Luke tried a long kick, Chris had already moved into position to repeat his earlier save. This time, however, Chris allowed the ball to squirm over the line.

"One to zero!" cried Luke. "Easy!"

Chris shook his head in dismay. He remembered the final line of the rhyme on the back of the Timewatch, and realized things could indeed work out both ways. "For better or worse."

Chapter 5

TIME FOR ACTION

"I can't say I didn't warn you, little brother," Becky said after dinner that night, as they strolled along the bank of the river. "Serves you right!"

Chris shrugged and tossed a stick into the early evening mist for Tan to fetch.

"I was just unlucky, that's all," he said. "Anybody can have an off day."

"True," said Becky. "But most people don't want to make it last even longer, do they?"

Chris sighed.

He wished that he hadn't told his twin about using, or misusing, the Timewatch to replay a game of soccer. "I've learned my lesson. I won't do it again," he said.

Becky was in a good mood after scoring a goal during her own team's game. She kept making fun of Chris because of a kick that flew past Chris into the top corner of the net. She would not let him forget it.

"I'm glad you didn't try to stop my goal," she said, grinning.

"By then, I was too mad," he mumbled. "I didn't care anymore."

They were quiet for a while, lost in thought. Only Tan's barking disturbed the peace and quiet by the river.

"It's weird, the way things can change," Chris said suddenly. "You know, how they can work out differently, if you have a second chance. It's like recording over something on a tape."

Becky thought about that for a few moments and then sighed. "Well, you can only do what you think is right at the time, even if that turns out to be wrong," she said. "Life's not a dress rehearsal. It's the real thing."

"Is it? I'm not so sure anymore," Chris replied. He switched his attention toward the farm on the edge of town. "Now that's what I call a big bonfire. Just look at those flames!"

Becky stared through the mist.

"The farmer must know what he's doing," she said.

"Not if his daughter has anything to do with it," Chris said with a smirk. "She isn't nicknamed Zany Zoe for nothing."

"Zoe's all right really," said Becky.

She paused, struggling to find the right word to describe Zoe's strange behavior at school. "She's just a little scatterbrained, that's all," she said finally.

"Scatterbrained!" Chris laughed. "She makes even Luke seem smart. Almost."

"Let's walk over to the farm and see if she's around," said Becky.

"Why?" asked Chris. "I didn't know you two were friends."

"We're not," Becky said. "I just want an excuse to go and stand next to that bonfire and get warm."

As the twins walked closer to the farm, however, the flames were shooting up even higher. They could hear people shouting and the noise of frightened animals.

"They might need help," Becky cried. "Come on! Run!"

Chris managed to grab Tan and put her on the leash to stop her chasing after his sister.

By the time he entered the farmyard, the fire was out of control and had spread to the barn. He could see two or three figures trying to put out the flames with hoses, but their work didn't seem to be helping.

Becky came racing back to Chris. "We've got to do something," she gasped. "Do you still have the watch?"

"Sure," said Chris, fishing it out of his coat pocket.

"Use it!" said Becky. "It sounds like there are animals trapped in the barn!"

"Is Zoe there?" asked Chris.

"I don't know," she said. "Just press that red button."

Click!

The next thing they knew, they were staring at each other in surprise across the kitchen table.

"Come on, you two, eat up," Mom told them. "You must both be starving after all that running around, playing soccer."

Becky looked down at her half-eaten meal and pushed the plate away. She had lost her appetite.

"What are we doing back here?" she asked her brother quietly.

"Having our supper again," Chris replied through a mouthful of food. "If you don't want yours, I'll have it."

"How can you eat at a time like this?" said Becky. "The farm's on fire!"

Chris shook his head and reached for her plate. "Not yet, it isn't, sis," he corrected her, pointing his fork at the kitchen clock and dropping a few beans onto the floor, which Tan licked up. "We've got plenty of time."

* * *

"Hi, guys!" Zoe greeted them, before throwing more wood onto the small bonfire in the farmyard. "What brings you here?"

"Um," Chris began, not quite sure what to say, since they had arrived at the farm a little early. "We were just out walking the dog."

"And doing a little jogging to keep in shape," added Becky.

"A dog jog!" Zoe joked.

"Not exactly," mumbled Chris. "So where is everybody?"

"Everybody?" asked Zoe. "Everywhere, I guess. Why?"

"I just wondered who's supposed to be taking care of this bonfire," he said.

"What's it look like?" she sneered. "I am, of course."

"Do your folks know?"

Zoe stared at him. "Of course they do. They don't call me zany here at home, you know."

Becky tried to come to Chris's rescue. "I'm sure you know what you're doing, Zoe," she said. "But isn't it dangerous having a bonfire so close to the barn?"

Zoe lost patience with their questions. "Go away," she snapped.

Zoe walked away toward her bike that was propped up against the barn. "I'm busy," she said.

The twins left the farm but did not walk very far.

"What do we do now?" asked Chris.

"We wait," said Becky. "I mean, we know what's going to happen, if we just leave her alone. So we'll wait a while and then move in."

"I don't want to stand here in the cold," said Chris. "Let's go take care of it now."

"Wait!" Becky cried. "What will we say to Zoe? Tell her she's going to set fire to the whole place? She'll just think we're crazy."

"So what?" said Chris. "It's better than frying the pigs. Come on!"

Chris marched back into the yard. Zoe was nowhere to be seen, and neither was her bike. The fire was still burning brightly.

"Wait here with Tan, Becky," he said, "and give me a shout if you see anybody."

"What are you going to do?"

"Put out that fire while I still can," he said over his shoulder.

Chris ran over to one of the farm's outbuildings, where he saw a hose connected to the wall. He turned on the tap and ran toward the bonfire, the length of hose unraveling behind him

The water began to gush out of the nozzle even before he reached the fire, drenching his jeans until he aimed it at the flames.

He quickly put out the fire. He soaked everything, trying to make sure the fire could not be relit, and then dropped the hose on the ground.

"I've done it!" he shouted in triumph. "Let's get out of here!"

As they headed home, they saw Zoe on her bike.

At first they thought she must be coming after them, but she turned off into one of the side streets toward the town square.

"Whew! That was close." Chris breathed in relief. "I'll bet she's angry, looking for us."

"Well, she knows where we live," Becky said. "And it's not that way."

"She must be going somewhere else, then," Chris replied.

"Hey! I bet that's how it happened before," he said. "She rode off and left the bonfire burning and, well, we know the rest."

Becky nodded. "Yes, but nobody else does, so let's just keep it to ourselves."

"All right," he said with a grin. "My lips are zipped!"

Chris made a quick motion with his hand across his mouth as if to seal it, but then immediately spoke again. "Too bad we can't tell her what we did, though."

He was cut short by screams and shouts in the distance.

"It's coming from the town square," said Becky, changing direction. "Let's go check it out."

Becky and Tan reached the square before Chris, who didn't want to run into Zoe again. Unluckily, somebody else already had.

Becky recognized Zoe's bike, even though it was smashed and lying in the gutter. She could see no sign of Zoe herself because of the crowd, but she soon found out what had happened.

"Zoe's been hit by a car!" she gasped as Chris caught up with her. "Use the watch. We might be able to save her."

Click!

Nothing changed. They were still in the square and they could still hear the wailing siren of an approaching ambulance.

"Try again!" cried Becky.

Click! Click!

"We're already in extra time, remember," Chris said, shaking his head. "Maybe the watch can't repeat the same hour twice."

The twins stood by, helpless, as the ambulance arrived in the square. It wasn't long before they saw a stretcher being carried into the back of the vehicle.

"Sorry, Zoe," Chris said. He sighed. "But at least we put the fire out for you."

Chapter 6

A MATTER OF TIME

"That poor girl," Mom said while the twins were having breakfast the next day. "It's a miracle that Zoe wasn't killed. Someone said the driver must have been doing at least sixty. He ought to be locked up."

The twins kept quiet, each lost in their own thoughts. They were glad that they'd prevented the fire, but they still wondered if they could have done anything to stop Zoe from being hurt.

There was a special assembly at school that morning to wish for Zoe's recovery, but it meant more to some than others.

"I saw you in assembly," sneered Luke, standing at Chris's locker at lunch. "Hands tight together, eyes shut, praying like mad."

"So? I just want Zoe to get better," Chris replied. "Don't you?"

Luke shrugged. "She always rides her bike like a maniac," he said. "It was only a matter of time before she got in an accident."

Only a matter of time.

The words stung and Chris could not stop himself. He grabbed Luke by the front of his shirt and shoved him back against the wall.

"What do you know about time?"
Chris asked fiercely. "Nothing!"

"What's your problem?" cried Luke,
wriggling out of his grip. "You're acting
as crazy as Zoe."

Chris scowled and trudged outside to
a corner of the schoolyard. He needed
more time to think. He wished he hadn't
left the Timewatch at home.

He was still in a bad mood that afternoon during art class. The teacher suggested that the students make or paint something that they could take to the hospital to show Zoe, which would cheer her up.

Becky still felt guilty, as if the accident were somehow their fault. She made a big, colorful card for Zoe, but it wasn't enough. She decided that the watch had to go.

"Maybe Zoe's accident wouldn't have happened if we hadn't interfered," she said to Chris when they were talking it over again after supper.

"Interfered?" he repeated, turning up the TV so that they couldn't be overheard from the store. "You mean, we shouldn't have done anything, and let the farm burn down?" he asked.

"No, course not," said Becky.

"Anyway, that speeding driver might have hit somebody else instead," said Chris.

"That's just it," his sister said. "All these weird possible effects of changing things. They're out of our control."

Chris spread his hands in a helpless gesture. "It's all luck," he said. "It's being in the wrong place at the wrong time."

"Yes, like us," she told him. "We've been in the wrong place too, going back and trying to put things right. Perhaps we made things worse."

"So what are you suggesting?"

"Destroy the Timewatch!" she said.

"What!" exclaimed Chris. "You can't be serious."

"I'm completely serious. It's more trouble than it's worth. Just imagine if someone like Luke got the watch and found out what it could do."

Chris refused to listen anymore. "I'm going out," he said. "On my own."

He went upstairs to get the Timewatch. He wanted to take it with him for safekeeping in case Becky tried to carry out her threat. He opened the top drawer of his dresser and looked through his socks and underwear. The watch wasn't there.

He yanked open the other drawers, and then he began to panic.

"Becky!" he cried, thundering down the stairs. "Where's the watch?"

He was too late.

Click!

* * *

Becky used the perfect escape route, slipping back in time. She was in the garden, playing ball with Tan again, while Chris was at a friend's house.

"Oh, well," she sighed, realizing that their argument had not yet taken place. "At least Chris doesn't know yet that I want to get rid of this thing."

She stared at the watch in her hand.

It was very tempting to go and throw it away, but she didn't really want to do anything like that without talking to him.

"Come on, Tan, let's go out for a little walk," she said. "We've got time."

"Don't be long," said Mom. "I'll be starting supper soon."

It began to rain before they reached the fields, and Becky decided to visit her aunt, who lived nearby, instead.

"This is a pleasant surprise," Auntie Jean greeted her. "Come in. We haven't had a good old chat for ages."

A big plate of cookies was on the table and Auntie Jean began to pour some milk, putting a bowl of water on the floor for Tan too.

"Can I call Mom to let her know where I am?" Becky asked.

"Of course, dear," said Auntie Jean. "The phone's in the hall."

Becky wanted to avoid going home for another meal, so she told Mom that she was having supper with Auntie Jean instead, which was mostly true. Supper and cookies!

When she returned to the kitchen, Auntie Jean handed her a plate. "Help yourself to the cookies, my dear, and tell me what you've been up to."

Becky was careful not to mention the watch and, instead, talked about events at school, boasting about her goals at yesterday's soccer practice.

"I don't know," said her aunt, shaking her head. "Girls playing soccer! It was never heard of in my day. Tennis, that was my favorite game."

Now it was Becky's turn to listen to Auntie Jean. Becky knew all her stories about playing for the school tennis team, but was content to sit back and enjoy the cookies.

When the grandfather clock struck six times, Auntie Jean looked alarmed.

"Oh, my goodness!" she exclaimed. "I forgot to buy a ticket."

"Ticket?" asked Becky.

"Yes, you know, for the Daily Draw."

"Oh, right, the lottery," said Becky. "It's okay, the store's still open."

"I'm afraid it's too late now, my dear. The deadline was six o'clock. Your uncle normally buys a ticket on his way home from work, but he's working overtime and asked me to get it today."

"Have you ever won anything?" asked Becky.

"Only twenty dollars, once," Auntie Jean said. "But I don't mind. Most of the money goes to support local charities and that's the main thing."

"How much is the top prize?"

"Right now it's ten thousand dollars," said Auntie Jean.

Becky whistled. "Wow! What would you do with all that money?" she asked. "Go on a world cruise or something?"

"Oh, no! Nothing so selfish," Auntie Jean chuckled. "We'd share our good fortune with the rest of the family. We always buy the same numbers, you see, like family birthdays."

When Tan started to bark they knew Uncle Dave was home from work.

"Not a word to your uncle about the ticket, remember," said Auntie Jean, pressing a finger to her lips. "He'll never know I forgot!"

As soon as Uncle Dave walked in, Tan gave him a loud, happy welcome.

Then more food appeared. Uncle Dave switched on the radio before settling himself in his favorite chair with the evening paper. "Let's check whether we've won the lottery!" he said, joking. "You never know, Becky, you might have brought us some good luck today!"

Becky exchanged a glance with her aunt and crossed her fingers.

There was no need for Uncle Dave to see the ticket. He knew the numbers by heart. He wasn't listening closely to the radio, but as the winning numbers were read out, some of them sounded familiar enough to gain his full attention. He stared at his wife, who had turned pale, and then he jumped to his feet.

"Come on!" he shouted at the radio. "Say them again!"

When the announcer repeated the five lucky numbers, Uncle Dave could hardly believe his ears. "We've won, Jean!" he cried, giving his wife a big hug as Tan added her barks to the excitement. "We won it! We got all five numbers!"

It was a few minutes before he had calmed down enough for his wife to tell him the bad news.

"I'm so sorry," she confessed. "With Becky here, I completely forgot to go and buy the ticket. I'm so sorry!"

Her husband was so shocked, he could not even find the words to respond.

He just shuffled out of the house and went into the back garden by himself.

Even Tan knew that something was wrong, and crouched under the table, her tail between her legs.

"I guess I'm not good luck," said Becky.

She knew that she could not use the watch again to repeat the past hour.

"It's not your fault, my dear," Auntie Jean told her, forcing a smile. "Just one of those things."

Becky put on her coat and walked slowly home with Tan. She felt terrible. She knew it was her fault.

But she also knew what else was to blame.

It was the Timewatch.

Chapter 7

TIME TRAVEL?

"We have to get rid of this thing," Becky insisted, "before it causes any more problems."

She had forgotten to take the Timewatch out of her coat last night. She handed it over to Chris in the school playground after lunch. She wanted nothing more to do with it.

"It stops things from turning out the way they were meant to," she told him.

"Meant?" Chris repeated, raising an eyebrow. "Who knows what's really supposed to happen?"

"We do," she replied. "Auntie Jean and Uncle Dave were supposed to win the lottery, and now they didn't because of that watch."

"And you and the cookies."

"Yes, all right, and me. Go ahead, rub it in, little brother," said Becky.

"Hey! Knock off the little brother stuff," Chris said, grinning. "I bet, with our own time trips, I've lived longer than you now by about an hour, little sister!"

Becky made a face at his teasing. She almost wished she hadn't told him what had happened. She had hoped that by telling him she would stop feeling so guilty, but she still felt terrible.

The only good news was that they had heard at assembly that Zoe was getting better.

"Let's smash the watch to pieces," Becky suggested.

Chris pushed the watch deep into his coat pocket, in case Becky tried to snatch it back and throw it to the ground. "We can't do that," he said.

"Why not?"

"Well, it might be the only watch in the world like this, that's why not. It just needs to be used properly. You know, to help people, like I did with Dad."

Becky could hardly argue with that. She turned away to walk back inside the building. Chris started kicking a ball around with some of the other boys.

"You can only play if you play goalie," said Butch. "I want to kick the ball for a change."

Chris was happy enough about that. He was better with his hands than his feet, even if he wasn't as good with either as Butch.

He took off his coat, folded it up tightly to protect the watch, and then placed it beneath a pile of other coats being used as goalposts.

Much to his surprise, Chris found himself playing really well. He even dived across the hard ground to stop one of Luke's shots.

"You see why Butch never dives out here," Luke sneered as Chris pulled up a sleeve to look at the bruise on his left elbow. "Bet you won't do it again."

Chris soon proved Luke wrong. He threw himself again to keep out another shot and Butch cheered.

"They say all goalies are crazy," Butch said, with a grin.

"Then that must include you, too," Chris joked back.

Soon the bell rang and the players ran for their coats.

Luke, with an unhappy look on his face, tossed Chris's coat to him.

"Hey!" cried Chris, catching the coat before it hit the ground. "I have something valuable in here."

"What?" asked Luke.

"None of your business. Just watch it." Chris grinned at his own pun as he brushed past Luke to head for the classroom.

The two boys continued to argue at their table throughout the afternoon and they were only quiet when Mr. Samuels gave everyone an unexpected spelling test. What was not unexpected, however, were the poor scores of both Chris and Luke.

The teacher ended the day with a story, grouping the children around him in the book corner, and it was only then that Chris realized Luke was missing.

Chris's mind immediately flashed to the Timewatch. He had thought about bringing it with him to class, but felt it might be safer, and less tempting to use, if he left it in his coat. He was now wishing he had brought it, and also feeling stupid for telling Luke that he had something valuable in his coat.

He waved his hand in the air to attract the teacher's attention.

"What is it now, Christopher?" sighed Mr. Samuels. "I suppose you're going to tell me that time travel isn't really possible."

Chris was surprised. "What?" he said, catching his twin's eye. He hadn't even been listening to the science fiction story about people traveling through time and space. He just wanted to leave the room.

"Well, what do you think?" Mr. Samuels asked.

"Um, I'm sure it is," said Chris.

"And why are you so sure?" asked Mr. Samuels, looking closely at Chris.

Becky shot Chris a warning look.

"Well, I just think it must be," Chris said. "I mean . . ."

Chris didn't get the chance to finish saying what he meant. "Ow!" he exclaimed, glaring at Luke, who had kicked him on the knee beneath their table. "Stop it, will you?"

For once, Luke wasn't smirking. His face had turned deathly pale. "What's up with you?" Chris asked, not really concerned.

"Everything's weird," Luke mumbled.

"You're weird," Chris told him and returned to his work.

Luke flicked a pencil at him. "I want to know what's going on around here. Don't try to fool me."

Chris stared at him. "I don't know what you're talking about."

Luke held out the Timewatch. "I'm talking about this."

"What are you doing with that?" Chris gasped. "Give it back."

"Not till you tell me what's going on," said Luke. "I just pressed this red button and then suddenly found myself back here. It's only two o'clock, but it should be almost time to go home."

"You've stolen that watch twice," Chris said, making a grab for it.

Luke was too quick. Chris leaned over the table and tried to take it back by force.

"Stop it, you two, right now!" shouted Mr. Samuels. "Come here!"

Even though he desperately wanted the watch back, Chris could not admit what started their latest fight. Both boys remained silent. The teacher sent them to sit in opposite corners of the room.

"Stay behind after school," Mr. Samuels told them. "We'll take care of this business then."

When the teacher announced the spelling test, only one pupil was not caught by surprise. Sitting alone, Luke had slowly realized what must have happened. He decided to make the best of his situation.

Knowing which words had come up in the test before, Luke checked in a dictionary and tried to memorize them.

Mr. Samuels was astonished by Luke's test. The boy had only two words wrong.

"This is remarkable, Luke," he said. "It shows what you are capable of when you put your mind to it. Perhaps you should sit by yourself more often."

Luke's grin became even wider when he found out that Chris had only half of the words right.

"Too bad it hasn't had the same effect on you, Christopher," said Mr. Samuels, frowning at him over his glasses.

Later on, in the book corner, when the teacher had finished reading the story about time travel, he asked the class a question:

"How many of you would like to travel back in time, if you had the chance?"

Most of the hands went up, including Luke's, which was the highest.

"Yes, Luke?" said Mr. Samuels, pleased to see some enthusiasm from him for a change. "And just where would you like to go back to?"

"It doesn't matter," Luke said, grinning. "Anywhere but here."

The children laughed, but the teacher was not amused.

"And do you think that time travel will ever be possible?" he asked.

"It already is," Luke said, and he held the Timewatch in the air, much to the twins' horror. "And I'll prove it. Look!"

Click!

Luke did not know that the same hour could not be repeated twice. He had made a big deal of pressing the red button, but nothing happened.

He clicked it again and again, but the students and Mr. Samuels were still all sitting together in the book corner, staring at him as if he were crazy.

"Yes, Luke, very dramatic," the teacher said. "Perhaps we can talk about that nonsense after school, too."

Luke slumped back against a bookcase, his face almost as red as the button on the Timewatch.

Chapter 8

OUT OF TIME

"So, how are we going to get the watch back from Luke?" asked Becky as the twins walked home.

"I don't know," Chris muttered. "He won't just give it back, that's for sure."

"I wonder when Luke will use the watch again," Becky said. "And what he will do with it?"

"He'll use it as soon as he can," Chris replied. "But as for what he'll do, your guess is as good as mine."

"Let's go find him," Becky said. She whistled for Tan to come join them. "Wherever he is."

Luke was still at home, which was the last place the twins thought of checking. They were sure he would be out somewhere, looking for mischief.

Luke watched television for a while till he got bored, and then went into the yard to kick a ball around.

It was only when the ball flew over the fence and broke a window in his neighbor's house that he decided to use the watch. His neighbor was storming out of the house.

Click!

After a moment of blurry vision and dizziness, it seemed as though the world around him had changed.

Luke found himself back in the town square, where he had briefly been at four o'clock on his way home, exactly one hour ago.

"Well, at least that window's still in one piece," he thought. Luke sat on the stone steps of the statue in the center of the busy square, wondering what to do next. That particular problem was solved by the arrival of Butch, but it led to a far more serious one.

"What was all that stuff in class with the watch?" asked Butch, sitting down next to him. "You made yourself look like an idiot."

Luke took the watch from his pocket and dangled it from the chain, swinging it back and forth in front of Butch's face as if trying to hypnotize him. "Can you keep a secret?" he asked.

Butch grinned. "Sure."

"Well, if you click the red button, this watch really does send you back in time," said Luke.

"Oh, yeah?" said Butch, pretending he believed Luke. "How far back?"

"One hour."

"One hour!" said Butch, unimpressed. "Is that the best you can do, just one measly hour?"

Butch snorted. "Give it here." He snatched the watch and jabbed at the red button. "Nothing's happening," he scoffed. "Nothing's changing."

But something had happened. The button was stuck. Butch tossed the watch back to Luke and stood up to leave.

"You broke it," Luke wailed.

"Tough! I'll see you later." Butch left the market and bumped into the twins just beyond the square.

"You haven't seen Luke lately, have you?" asked Chris.

"Funny you should say that," Butch replied, bending over to pet Tan. "I just saw him at the statue. The weirdo was still trying to pretend his watch is some kind of time machine!"

"Does he still have it?" asked Becky.

"Yeah, but it can't even tell time now." Butch chuckled. "It's broken."

"Broken!" exclaimed Chris.

"The red button's jammed," he told them with a laugh. "Serves him right, if you ask me. See ya!"

The twins looked at each other in alarm and hurried into the square.

There was no sign of Luke. "Where do you think he is now?" asked Chris.

"Let's try the field," Becky suggested. "He might have run over there."

To their dismay, the field was empty, but they continued their search by the river.

Suddenly, Becky yelled, "There he is!" She was pointing toward the train track. Chris spotted Luke, too.

Luke was climbing over the fence on the opposite side of the track and then disappeared into a set of trees.

Chris grabbed Tan's collar to attach her leash, while Becky started racing through the long grass, leaving them both far behind.

As Becky neared the track, she saw what Luke had done.

She turned and shouted back to her brother, "Chris! He put a big branch on the track!"

The words were barely out of her mouth when they heard the loud whistle of a train, a warning to anyone who might be on the path that crossed the track. Trains didn't come down this stretch of track very often, but Luke must have known that one was due.

Only someone as fast as Becky would have been able to reach the crossing before the train.

She jumped over the fence and screeched to a halt in the gravel by the track, her heart pounding. With the train closing rapidly upon her, its noise filling her senses, she grabbed hold of the heavy branch and pulled.

Chris was still too far away to help and a long, rattling line of trucks blocked his view of the path, drowning Tan's barks and his own desperate cries.

"Becky!" he screamed. "Becky!"

Chapter 9

TIME LOOP

Chris stared in horror as the trucks clanked by. He was scared to think what he might see when they had all gone past.

The sight was the one he dreaded. His sister was face down, lying very still.

"Becky!" he cried.

To his huge relief, she slowly rolled over and sat up, her face smeared with dirt.

"I'm okay," she croaked. "What took you so long, little brother?"

Chris shook his head. "That was a stupid thing to do," he told her. "You could've been killed."

Becky scrambled to her feet to escape Tan licking her face. "I know. I realize that now. Sorry," she said, feeling a little dizzy. "At least I saved the driver from getting hurt, if the train had been derailed or something."

"True," Chris admitted. "So now let's get Luke before he tries anything else like that."

"Why would he do such a thing?" Becky said as they set off toward the woods, where Luke had run off. "It doesn't make sense. Even for him."

* * *

There was no escape for Luke from his living nightmare.

With the red button jammed, he was trapped in a time loop. He kept having to repeat the same hour. Every time the little gold arrow completed a circuit of the dial, it began to move slowly around all over again.

By the third loop, Luke was becoming desperate. He panicked, though, when he heard Becky's shout and threw the branch onto the tracks.

Luke had already vented his frustration in other ways. Returning to school, he scratched Mr. Samuels's car with a nail, stole a ball from the locker room, tipped over garbage cans, and smashed several classroom windows.

The twins were following his trail of damage all over town. He was hard to catch.

They had no idea that he was stuck in a loop and kept returning to various places, like the farm, where he let pigs and hens out into the yard. Or the new housing area, where he damaged doors, flowers, trees, cars, and more windows.

Finally, Luke got tired of breaking things. He went to sit by the river for a while to think.

"Maybe none of it really happened," he thought, trying to comfort himself that each extra hour simply erased what he had done before. Luke began to throw stones into the water, using some ducks as targets, and didn't hear the twins sneak up behind him.

"Got you!" Chris cried out.

"What are you doing here?" Luke said, trying to act cool.

"What were you doing back there on the train track?" asked Becky. "You almost caused a wreck."

Luke shrugged. "Who cares?"

"We do," said Becky.

"So? What do you want?"

"The watch," she said simply.

Luke shrugged again. "It's broken."

"We know," said Chris. "Butch told us. But we still want it back."

Luke took the watch from his coat pocket and glared at it. "Thanks to Butch, I'm stuck in a kind of time loop," he said. "There's no way out. I'm just going around in circles."

Angrily, Luke threw the watch at a duck on the bank, but his aim was bad and the watch flew into the river.

"You want it, you fetch it!" he cried.

At the word "fetch," Tan ran away and jumped into the shallow water.

"Good girl!" Becky shouted. "Find it, Tan!"

A few moments later, Tan's head bobbed beneath the surface and reappeared with the watch hanging from her mouth by the chain.

Becky praised Tan again. "Good girl!"

Tan paddled to the bank, climbed out, and shook herself, spraying Luke with water. Then she dropped the watch at Chris's feet.

Chris picked it up and peered at the tiny gold arrow. "Must be waterproof. It still seems to be working," he said. But he pressed the red button, and it refused to budge.

"What time is it when you slip back?" Becky asked Luke.

"Five o'clock," he muttered.

Becky glanced at her wristwatch.

"It's almost five now," she told Chris. "What can we do?"

"I don't know," he said, "but we've got to do something."

Chris looked like he had made a decision. He walked to the water's edge, leaned over, and scooped up a large stone from the riverbed.

Luke suddenly realized what Chris had in mind. "No! Don't!" he yelled. "You don't know what . . ."

Too late!

Chris's hand came down hard, slamming the stone onto the Timewatch and breaking its glass front. The gold arrow crunched and the red button snapped back up into place.

"Look what you've done!" cried Luke.

"Just wait!" Chris told him. "Then we'll see what I've done."

The three of them seemed to be holding their breaths.

Tan wandered away to start rolling in the grass to dry her fur.

After what seemed like years, the church clock began to strike the hour. They counted the bongs out loud.

"That's five," Chris said. "If anything was going to happen, Luke, you'd be back in the market square again by now. You're free at last."

Luke let out a sigh of relief. "I thought about smashing the watch myself, but I couldn't," he said.

"I don't think I could have, either, if it'd been me," Chris replied. "It just seemed like the only thing to do."

They stared at the broken watch on the ground.

"What do we do with it now?" Luke asked. "Throw it back in the water?'"

"No, we'd better destroy the Timewatch once and for all," said Becky.

She picked up the watch and said, "We'll make sure nobody can ever use it again."

"Or misuse it," added Chris, glancing at Luke.

"I'm really going to enjoy this," Becky said, kneeling down. "I've been wanting to do this forever."

She hammered the stone onto the watch, shattering it into a hundred tiny pieces. "There!" she said, standing up. "Now Luke can pick up all the pieces and we can go home."

Luke picked up the pieces without any argument. Then he tossed them into the river before they could stop him.

Chris whistled for Tan and winked at his sister.

"Of course, there's still one more thing you have to do, Luke," he said with a smirk.

"Yeah?" said Luke. "What's that?"

"Start thinking what you might say to people about all the things you did this past hour," Chris told him. "That hasn't been wiped out, remember?"

ABOUT THE AUTHOR

Before Rob Childs wrote his first book, he taught children for 20 years. One of his favorite experiences as a teacher was being able to coach soccer and gymnastics. Childs eventually wrote more than 80 books for children, including a popular series of sports books. He also wrote a series called *Time Rangers* for Scholastic. Childs lives with his wife, Joy, and their collie dog, Rocky. Rocky likes to take Childs for walks in the nearby countryside.

ABOUT THE ILLUSTRATOR

One of Nicola Slater's favorite pasttimes is to make monkeys out of socks. She became an illustrator so that she could spend her days lounging around her house drawing silly pictures. She lives in England and claims that she can levitate household objects with her mind.

GLOSSARY

boasted (BOHST-id)—bragged

decisive (di-SYE-siv)—making a decision clearly and firmly

derail (di-RAYL)—to run or cause to run off the rails (of a train track)

dramatic (druh-MAT-ik)—full of action and excitement

flea market (FLEE MAR-kit)—a place for selling items

hypnotize (HIP-nuh-tize)—to put someone into a sleep-like condition. A person who is hypnotized will usually obey the commands of the hypnotizer.

restock (re-STOK)—to put out more supplies and goods for sale

rickety (RIK-uh-tee)—likely to break or fall apart; shaky

scatterbrained (SKAT-ur-braynd)—regarded as flighty, thoughtless, or disorganized

suspicious (suh-SPISH-uss)—acting in a way that seems wrong or untrustworthy

DISCUSSION QUESTIONS

1. Would you like to travel back in time? What would you do? When and where would you go? Explain your answers.

2. Do you think that the characters in this story should have interfered with time? Why or why not?

3. On page 61, Luke says "it was only a matter of time . . ." What is meant by this phrase? Chris's dad says that "Time is money." What does that saying mean?

WRITING PROMPTS

1. Chris begins to think of ways that he might use the timewatch. Make a list of the ways you would use a magic timewatch, if you discovered one.

2. Write about how you use an extra hour in your day. What hour would you like to repeat and why?

3. If the red button on the watch was held down for a long time, would the twins travel further back in time? Write a story where the twins travel to another time period.

INTERNET SITES

Do you want to know more about subjects related to this book? Or are you interested in learning about other topics? Then check out FactHound, a fun, easy way to find Internet sites.

Our investigative staff has already sniffed out great sites for you!

Here's how to use FactHound:

1. Visit *www.facthound.com*

2. Select your grade level.

3. To learn more about subjects related to this book, type in the book's ISBN number: **1598891162**.

4. Click the **Fetch It** button.

FactHound will fetch the best Internet sites for you!